08/2015

D0057879

# CLEANUP

BOWEN ISLAND PUBLIC LIBRARY

# NORAH McCLINTOCK
# CLEANUP

RAVEN BOOKS
*an imprint of*
ORCA BOOK PUBLISHERS

Copyright © 2012 Norah McClintock

All rights reserved. No part of this publication may be reproduced
or transmitted in any form or by any means, electronic or mechanical,
including photocopying, recording or by any information storage
and retrieval system now known or to be invented, without permission
in writing from the publisher.

**Library and Archives Canada Cataloguing in Publication**

McClintock, Norah
Cleanup / Norah McClintock.
(Rapid reads)

Issued also in electronic formats.
ISBN 978-1-4598-0054-0

I. Title.  II. Series: Rapid reads
PS8575.C62C54 2012      C813'.54      C2012-902260-8

First published in the United States, 2012
**Library of Congress Control Number:** 2012944097

**Summary:** When an illegal alien working as a maid is charged with
her employer's murder, her only friend is also her only hope
for escaping jail or worse, deportation. (RL 4.0)

*Orca Book Publishers is dedicated to preserving the environment and has
printed this book on paper certified by the Forest Stewardship Council®.*

Orca Book Publishers gratefully acknowledges the support for
its publishing programs provided by the following agencies:
the Government of Canada through the Canada Book Fund and the
Canada Council for the Arts, and the Province of British Columbia
through the BC Arts Council and the Book Publishing Tax Credit.

Design by Teresa Bubela
Cover photography by Getty Images

ORCA BOOK PUBLISHERS
PO Box 5626, Stn. B
Victoria, BC Canada
V8R 6S4

ORCA BOOK PUBLISHERS
PO Box 468
Custer, WA USA
98240-0468

www.orcabook.com
Printed and bound in Canada.

15 14 13 12 • 4 3 2 1

*For Sarah and everyone else*
*who cleans up other people's messes.*

# CHAPTER ONE

Maria called me before I got out of bed. She said I didn't have to pick her up. She would get to work on her own.

I should have known something was going on. But I didn't give it any thought. I liked Maria. She was the only person I knew that I could speak to in Spanish. She was alone in the country. And she was lonely, like a lot of illegal immigrants. She was on the run from gangsters back in Colombia. I had tried to convince her to make a claim for refugee status. But she was terrified of being denied and being deported. I felt sorry for her.

But aside from being newcomers and co-workers, we had little in common. Maria liked to chatter about all the things she was going to have one day. "You have to think positive, no, Connie?" The things she wanted were things she had seen on TV or in out-of-date magazines she bought at the library for ten cents each. They were things like shoes and purses, dresses and jewelry—things I used to have.

Things I told myself I didn't miss.

I double-checked the two trays of cleaning supplies in the trunk of the beat-up Toyota hatchback that I'd bought for next to nothing—but still on installment—after six months of taking the bus. I put my thermos of coffee, my sandwich and my piece of fruit on the front seat. Then I drove north, to one of the city's wealthiest neighborhoods.

The gates across the driveway of Mr. Withers's house were open. So was the side door, the one Maria and I used. Usually the gates were closed and the door was locked.

Frowning, I nudged the door with one shoulder and poked my head in. "Missy Maid!" I called.

That's not my name. It's the name of the company I work for. My name is Connie, short for Consuela.

Mr. Richard Withers, the owner of the house, didn't appear from the kitchen the way he did every morning when Maria and I arrived. He was a distinguished-looking old gentleman who lived alone except for a cook who came in from ten in the morning until five in the afternoon every day to prepare his meals. He had an easy smile, and when he handed over his list of tasks, he always said "please" or "if you don't mind."

But he didn't answer my call that day. Instead, Maria did, in panicky Spanish.

"Connie, thank God. I don't know what to do. I think he's dead."

"Where are you?" I shouted.

"Up here. In the bedroom."

The bedroom? What was she doing up there?

I dropped my two trays of cleaning supplies and hurried through the mudroom, which I doubt had ever seen any mud. I ran through the kitchen and up the back stairs to the second floor.

Richard Withers was in his early seventies. He had had a heart attack when he was sixty and had been careful ever since. He ate sensibly and exercised regularly, as was obvious from his lean build. But I knew about heart disease—two of my uncles had died from it. So I expected to find that Mr. Withers had had a second, fatal, attack during the night. Poor man, dying all alone, I thought.

That's why I wasn't prepared for the scene that greeted me.

It was clear that Richard Withers had not died of a heart attack. Nor had he died alone. Not unless he had bludgeoned himself over the head with the foot-high brass angel that was lying in a pool of blood beside his motionless body.

# CHAPTER TWO

Maria stood next to the body. Her large black eyes were fixed on the old man's face. Her cinnamon skin had a chalky hue. Blood stained her hands. The sheets were tangled on the bed. A pillow lay on the floor. Artificial scents filled the air—shampoo and soap, perfume and men's cologne—and I felt myself becoming congested. But, for once, I didn't worry about my allergies. I was too stunned by the sight of Mr. Withers lying on the floor in front of me.

Questions for Maria exploded in my head: What happened? When did you find him?

How did you find him? What are you doing up here? Who hit him? Did *you* hit him?

But the one that actually came out of my mouth was, "Why is your hair wet?"

Her hand went to her head. "Connie, I don't know what to do."

"Maria, you didn't…" I let my voice trail off and nodded at the body and the blood.

Maria's eyes widened in horror.

"No! No, never! I like Mr. Richard. I found him like that," she said.

I believed her. She had always spoken fondly of the old man and had even flirted with him. He had always responded eagerly.

"Did you call nine-one-one?"

The question seemed to jar her out of her shock.

"Nine-one-one brings the police," she said.

"Exactly. And the paramedics. And a fire truck—"

Oh.

"Did anyone see you arrive?" I asked. The question I didn't ask: *When* did you arrive?

She shook her head.

"I don't think so. I'm always careful."

Always? What did she mean by that?

"You have to go," I told her. "Right now, before anyone sees you."

If she hadn't done anything wrong, there was no reason for her to suffer. And she would definitely suffer if the police started to question her.

Maria didn't argue with me. She pulled a sweater from the foot of the bed.

"Go the back way, through the back garden," I said. "You can get into the ravine from there."

She nodded and reached for her purse, which was on the dresser, its contents strewn around it. She scooped everything into it with one hand.

"And, Maria, if you run into anyone or if anyone asks, you called me this morning

to tell me you weren't feeling well, okay?"
I said. "You didn't come into work. Call me
later. Promise?"

Maria hurried from the room. I waited
until I heard the back door open and close
again. Then I pulled out my cell phone and
punched in 9-1-1. It was only after I finished
the call that I noticed the key chain on the
floor near the dresser. It wasn't Mr. Withers's.
He kept his keys on a sterling silver ring with
his initials on it. They had to be Maria's. They
must have fallen off the dresser. I hesitated.
This was a crime scene. I knew better than to
move objects. But Maria had said she hadn't
done anything, and I believed her. I grabbed
the keys and dropped them into my pocket.

\* \* \*

I knew there were going to be questions.
Lots of them. I was right.

The first person to ask them was a young
police officer in uniform. I answered every

one of his questions even though my head was pounding and my sinuses were starting to close up. Later, in the hall outside the bedroom, a tall homicide detective named Bodie asked me the same questions all over again.

"Did you touch anything?" His eyes searched mine as if he were trying to read my soul. He spoke slowly and pronounced each word carefully, as if he thought my accent meant that my English was shaky. It wasn't.

"I touched the…him. I felt for a pulse," I said. My head was spinning by then. "Do you mind if I sit down?"

Bodie gestured to a couple of armchairs at the end of the hall in front of a floor-to-ceiling window. I sank onto one of them and pulled an inhaler out of my uniform pocket.

"You have asthma?" His eyes went to my wrist. I wear a MedicAlert bracelet.

"I have allergies," I said. "To strong artificial scents. Perfumes, detergents, air fresheners. That sort of thing."

"But you work as a house cleaner," he said.

"The agency I work for uses all-natural products." It was a strong selling point for Missy Maids.

"What about your clients? What if they wear scents?"

I held up my inhaler. "I manage," I said. "Please go on."

He hesitated, but only for a moment.

"Did you touch anything besides the body? The phone, for instance?" There was a cordless phone on the bedside table.

"I used my cell phone," I said.

"Did you see or hear anyone in the house before or after you found Mr. Withers?"

I knew it was important to answer this question without hesitating. But I hesitated anyway.

11

"Ms. Suarez?" Bodie said.

"Sorry." I did my best to look apologetic. "I just—"

I let the words hang as if they had frozen in midair. I glanced at the bedroom door and shuddered. Bodie had probably seen a lot of dead bodies, but I hadn't. I hoped that he would think I was rattled by the sight.

He repeated his question in the same no-nonsense tone. I reminded myself that he had also probably spoken to lots of witnesses and suspects—and murderers.

"No," I said. "I didn't see or hear anyone. Or anything."

"Does anyone else live in the house?" he asked.

"No."

"Servants?"

"There's a cook, but she doesn't live in," I said. I told him what I knew about

Mrs. Branch, which wasn't much. She stayed in the kitchen. She served and prepared lunch for Mr. Withers every day. She set out snacks of fruit and yogurt. And she prepared his dinner but didn't stay to serve it. Her day ended promptly at five.

"How often are you here?" Detective Bodie asked.

"Every day. I mean, every weekday."

He raised an eyebrow.

"Every day?" he said. "That's a lot of cleaning up after one man."

"It's a big house," I said. But that wasn't the real reason Maria and I were here so often. "I think Mr. Withers liked the company. I think he was lonely."

"He was a wealthy man," the detective said. "And you're telling me he was lonely?"

"He liked to talk. I guess he liked someone around to talk to."

"And it was just you?"

"Pardon?" I wasn't sure what he meant.

"Are you the only person who comes in to clean and to...talk?" he asked.

I thought about saying yes, but the police aren't stupid. Sooner or later Bodie would ask who I worked for. He would contact the agency and its owner Mike Czernecki. Mike would tell them that he had assigned two maids to the Withers house. Besides, I had lied enough.

"There's another girl," I said. "We usually come together."

"Usually?" Bodie said. "Where is she now?"

"She called me this morning to tell me she couldn't come in today."

"So she wasn't here?"

Hadn't I just said that? Was he trying to trip me up?

"No," I said. "She wasn't."

"So you're saying that you were the only one who came in this morning?"

The way he asked the question—and the fact that he asked it—made me nervous. Did he doubt me?

I nodded.

"The other girl," he said. "What's her name?"

"Maria Gonzales. We work for Missy Maids." I gave him Mike Czernecki's name.

# CHAPTER THREE

Detective Bodie asked more questions. When a forensics team showed up, he had them fingerprint me and asked for permission to take a cheek swab for DNA.

"We need to know what's what when we process the room," he said. In other words, he wanted to know if I had anything to do with Mr. Withers's murder.

I knew I could have said no, but I didn't. After that, he let me go.

I thought about calling Mike Czernecki on the way home and telling him that the police would be coming to see him.

And that he'd lost a good customer. In the end, I decided to leave that to Bodie. I would check in with Mike later. I went home and waited to hear from Maria.

She didn't call.

After I was sure that the police must have talked to Mike, I reached for my phone. Without Mr. Withers, I didn't have steady work anymore. And I couldn't afford to lose more than a couple of days' pay.

"Mike?"

"Yeah?" He growled as usual, like a mean old bear ready to attack. I pictured his burly body jammed in behind the desk in the closet-sized office that he called the nerve center of Missy Maids. I was sure he was scowling. Mike was always scowling.

"It's me," I said. "Connie."

I heard only silence on the other end of the line.

"I guess you heard what happened to Mr. Withers," I said.

"The cops were just here." He sounded grumpier than usual. "When were you going to tell me, Connie? Or *were* you going to tell me?"

"Of course I was going to tell you," I said. He was probably worried about the reputation of his company. "I'm sorry. I should have called you as soon as I got home."

I hate apologizing when I haven't done anything wrong. A few years ago, I never would have done it. But I was getting used to it. I had no choice. After being downsized out of my job as a legal assistant, the only work I had been able to find was non-skilled work paying minimum wage.

Like working for Mike's maid service.

Those jobs, I had learned, involved a lot of kissing ass—"Yes, ma'am," "No, sir," "Of course you're right, ma'am." I had wondered more than once if Serafina, our maid back home, had felt the same way toward my parents, her employers, as I felt toward Mike and the clients he sent me to work for.

"But I thought the police—" I continued.

"Screw the police," Mike snarled. "I'm talking about Maria. When were you going to tell me she was working off the books?"

"What?" What was he talking about?

"Don't play me, Connie. Not if you want to keep your job."

"I'm not playing you. What do you mean, Maria was working off the books?"

"Right. Like you don't know."

"But I don't," I protested.

"You don't know that she waltzed in here a month ago and told me she quit? Give me a break, Connie. You don't build a business by being the dullest knife in the drawer. The cops told me what you said to them—that you and Maria were working for Withers five days a week. Give me one good reason why I shouldn't fire your ass right now."

"What do you mean, she quit?"

I must have sounded as surprised as I felt, because instead of ranting at me, he was silent.

"You're telling me you didn't know?" he asked finally. His voice was heavy with suspicion.

"No. I didn't."

"That little gold digger didn't tell you?"

"No. And, by the way, neither did you." Wait a minute. "What do you mean, gold digger?"

I heard a snort on the other end of the line.

"You're kidding me, right, Connie?" Mike said.

I took a deep breath. I reminded myself that I *needed* this job. None of the law firms that I had approached in the past year were hiring legal secretaries—even ones who, like me, had a law degree, even if it was from a foreign country. Many of them were laying people off. Most of the places that were hiring—stores, hotels and maid services—had no interest in someone who had recently been a legal secretary. They wanted dumb, unskilled people who wouldn't make a fuss. I had found that out the hard way. I started leaving my legal secretary job off application forms the same as I had left off my law degree when I realized that most law firms didn't want a legal secretary who knew as much as, if not more than, her boss.

Mike, however, had guessed the truth.

"I've met plenty of girls from your neck of the woods," he had told me as he looked over my application. "Most of them don't speak English as good as you do. They sure as hell don't spell as good as you. So, what were you back home—a doctor? An engineer? A lawyer?" He watched my face the whole time, and nodded. "Lawyer, huh? I knew it had to be something like that."

"So you're not going to hire me?"

"Not hire you?" He looked at me as if I were crazy. "Hell, yeah, I'm going to hire you. Welcome to the American dream, sweetheart."

If I wanted Mike to find me another job, then I had to be nice. But I also wanted an answer.

"What do you mean, Maria is a gold digger?" I asked him again.

"Come on, Connie. I'm not stupid."

"Mike, I swear I don't know what you're talking about."

"Maria," he said. "I'm talking about Maria. When I hired her, she told me the neighborhoods where she was prepared to work. *Prepared* to work, mind you, like she was calling the shots. Don't give me lazy bourgeois housewives, she said. What does that even mean, bourgeois?"

I kept my mouth shut. I knew Mike well enough to know when he wanted an answer and when he didn't.

"She wanted rich neighborhoods and what she called mansions," he continued. "She wanted bachelors and widowers. Especially widowers."

I don't know what surprised me more—that she had said those things to Mike or that I hadn't known.

"And that's what you gave her, just because she asked?"

"I gave her Withers," he said, as if that explained everything. "You know how many maids I've sent Withers over the years? Dozens. Think about it, Connie. The man wanted two maids five days a week. That doesn't scream obsessive clean-freak to you? When Maria quit, I figured that he had finally broken her the way he'd broken all the others—except you."

I thought about the way Mr. Withers smiled whenever he encountered us on his rounds. I recalled the respectful tone he used when he handed over his list of assignments to Maria—always Maria—every day. He seemed almost apologetic, unlike many Missy Maids clients who seemed to enjoy bossing people around.

"Are we talking about the same person, Mike?" I asked. "Richard Withers?"

"The old coot? Yeah. I was surprised she lasted as long as she did. Then she quit and I thought good riddance. That dame was high-maintenance. Now I find out she didn't quit at all. She was still working for him, only off the books. That's a no-no, Connie. Check your contract. I wouldn't be surprised if that little tramp was banging the old man."

I thought about Maria's wet hair and the way she had said she was "always" careful.

"Did you tell the police that, Mike?" I asked.

"Damn right I did."

Mike promised to find me more work. He also said, "But if I find out that you knew about Maria and you didn't tell me, you're through. You got that?"

I said I did. And I vowed to use every minute that I wasn't working to look for a new job—one where I didn't have to take orders or give them. One where I could help people. Maybe something in immigration settlement or helping low-paid workers.

Definitely one where I wouldn't have to put up with Mike Czernecki.

\* \* \*

The next morning, I still hadn't heard from Maria—or Mike. It was so noisy outside my apartment door that I couldn't think. The building management was making improvements. Putting new floors in the kitchens and bathrooms as well as new countertops. Everyone was afraid they were going to raise the rent after they finished. If they did, I would have to move.

It was one more reason for me to start looking for a new job.

I grabbed my decade-old Prada—a gift from my parents in the good old days—and glanced in the mirror. I hadn't had a decent haircut in months, and it showed. But there was nothing I could do about that now. As I locked my apartment door, I saw workmen going in and out of the two apartments at the far end of the hall. They would get to my apartment soon.

I walked to the public library a few blocks away and booked time on a computer. I was searching job openings online when my cell phone vibrated. The display read PRIVATE NUMBER. Someone didn't want me to know who was calling.

I glanced at the computer. If I left now, I might not get it back again for hours. With a sigh, I shoved my pen and notebook into my purse and stood up.

"Hello?" I said, heading for the exit.

"Connie, you have to help me," a breathless voice said in Spanish.

Maria.

# CHAPTER FOUR

"**W**here are you?" I asked.

"At a police station. They arrested me. They said I could call a lawyer, so I called you, Connie."

"Yes, but—"

"They think I killed Mr. Richard. You have to tell them I would never do such a thing."

"But, Maria—"

She interrupted me to tell me which police station she was in. She begged me to hurry. Then the phone went dead.

I stood where I was for a few moments, thinking about the Maria I knew and the

Maria that Mike had told me about. Mike said she had her sights set on a rich man. A lot of women did, even if they never admitted it. Mike said she had quit the agency, and she hadn't told me. But not telling someone something wasn't the same as lying. And no matter how I looked at it, I couldn't see that Maria had anything to gain by killing Mr. Withers. And I couldn't imagine her beating him—or anyone else—to death.

I called one of my former co-workers, a legal assistant who worked for a criminal lawyer.

"He's in court, Connie," she said. "I can't reach him. But I'll let him know as soon as I can, okay?"

"Thanks, Emma." I gave her Maria's full name, the name of the detective on her case, and the station where she was being held. "I really appreciate this."

"No problem, kiddo," she said. That always made me smile. She was twenty-six.

I was five years older than her. "Hey, where are you working these days?"

"I'm between jobs at the moment," I said. Technically, it was the truth. "Oh, and Emma, my friend is Spanish-speaking, so if your boss needs a translator—"

"He will," she said. "I don't suppose you could do it?" When I hesitated, she said, "He'll pay you for your time."

And bill Maria, I thought. "It's probably a legal-aid case, Emma."

I heard her sigh. "He's still going to need a translator," she said.

"I'll give you my number. He can call me if he needs me."

\* \* \*

I was at home, staring at the TV and not caring that Rosie O'Donnell was drowned out by the hammering and the loud voices of the workmen down the hall, when Emma's boss called. His name was Gregory Mason. I told him what I knew.

"Emma said you can translate," he said. "Can I pick you up?"

I told him it would be faster if I met him at the police station. I was nearly there before I realized that I had left Maria's keys in my uniform pocket. If they released her, I would have to go all the way back home to get them.

I had no trouble spotting Gregory Mason. I'd seen him in the building where I used to work. He got out of a silver Lexus and strode up to the police station in the mainly immigrant neighborhood south of Richard Withers's house. To my surprise, he recognized me.

"You're just as Emma described," he said. "Thanks for coming. Does Ms. Gonzales speak any English?"

"Yes," I said. "But she's much more fluent in Spanish."

"Okay. Then we'll do it in Spanish. I want the whole story. I don't want her to have to struggle to get it out. Come on."

I hesitated.

"Did Emma tell you it will probably be a legal-aid case?" I asked. "Maria has been working as a house cleaner."

His smile was polished. "Let's not worry about that until we see what we're up against, okay?"

He led the way through the door and marched straight to the desk sergeant where he identified himself as Maria's lawyer and me as his translator.

A uniformed police officer was summoned to take us to an interview room. He knocked on the door, and Detective Bodie stepped out. Mr. Mason went through his introductions again. The whole time, Bodie looked disapprovingly at me.

"Ms. Suarez was at the scene," he told Mr. Mason.

"I understand she was the one who called nine-one-one," Mr. Mason said. "Is there a problem? Is she a suspect?"

"Not at this time, no."

"Is she being looked at as a possible suspect?" Mr. Mason asked.

"No," Bodie admitted.

"Well then, my translator and I would like to see Ms. Gonzales."

Bodie opened the door for us. Maria stood up when she saw me. She hugged me.

She waited until the detective had left before she said in Spanish, "I'm scared. They think I killed Mr. Richard."

I let her hug me again. Then I stepped back so that I could look at her and reassure myself that I was right to believe her.

Mr. Mason closed the door, introduced himself to Maria and explained why I was there. He asked his questions in English, speaking directly to Maria. Maria answered in Spanish. I translated.

"Tell me everything you can remember about that morning, Ms. Gonzales," Mr. Mason said. "Where you were, what you did, who you spoke to. Anything you can remember."

Maria looked down at the table while she spoke.

"I got up and went to the shower," she said hesitantly.

"No, I mean tell me everything from the time you arrived at Mr. Withers's house that morning," Mr. Mason said.

Maria's cheeks turned pink.

"I—I did not arrive in the morning." She refused to look at me but peeked at Mr. Mason. "I was there since the night before."

Mr. Mason raised an eyebrow when I translated her answer. So Mike was right, I thought. Maria had been having an affair with Mr. Withers.

"I see," Mr. Mason said. "Am I to gather that you and Mr. Withers were…involved?"

Maria's cheeks turned from pink to crimson.

"He was a good man," she said. "When he found out how much the agency was paying me, he said I should quit. He said he would pay me directly. He said he would pay me what I deserved." She turned to me and lowered her voice. "Mike paid me less than he paid you, because of my status."

I didn't translate the last part. Mr. Mason didn't seem to notice.

"Ms. Gonzales," he said, his eyes on Maria again, "about Mr. Withers…"

"We were going to get married," she said.

Married? I was stunned. When had that happened?

All that Mr. Mason said was, "I see." If he was surprised, he gave no sign of it. "Now, about the morning in question…"

Maria said that she had woken up at six o'clock, when Mr. Withers got out of bed.

He was an early riser. But he urged her to go back to sleep. He also told her that she should stop worrying about cleaning the house.

"He said you could do it, Connie," she said. "He said he would pay you extra, maybe hire you himself full time to work for him, never mind Mike. I told him you weren't a maid, Connie. Not really. He said he would help you. He said he could tell you are very smart. He knows many people."

Mr. Mason made notes with a fountain pen.

"I went back to sleep," Maria continued. "I didn't wake up until nearly two hours later when he came back into the bedroom. He was upset. I asked him what the matter was, but he said it was nothing for me to worry about."

Mr. Withers told her he had a few things to attend to. He went downstairs, and she got up to have a shower.

"You've seen the bathroom," Maria said to me. "We've scrubbed it often enough. The shower is wonderful. It's like standing under a waterfall, except the water is so hot. No one tells you to hurry up. No one pounds on the door. No one tells you not to waste the water or how high the electric bill will be. I could shower all day if I wanted and Mr. Richard would never say anything."

"How long were you in the shower?" Mr. Mason asked.

"Fifteen minutes. Twenty. I'm not sure. When I opened the bathroom door, I saw Mr. Richard lying on the bedroom floor." Tears welled up in her eyes. "He wasn't moving."

"What did you do then?" Mr. Mason asked.

Maria was silent.

"Maria," I said. "You have to answer."

She looked at me. Tears ran down her face.

"I'm so ashamed," she said.

"What did you do after you saw Mr. Withers lying on the bathroom floor?" Mr. Mason asked again, gently but firmly.

Maria hung her head. Her voice was no more than a whisper.

"I locked myself in the bathroom," she said. "I was afraid there was a thief in the house. I thought Mr. Richard must have surprised him." She wiped the tears from her cheeks with the backs of her hands. "I thought if he saw me, he would kill me too."

"How long were you in the bathroom that time?" Mr. Mason asked.

"I don't know. Ten minutes. Maybe more. I stayed there until I was sure I couldn't hear anything. When I came out, I called Connie."

"Why Connie?" Mr. Mason asked. "Why not the police? Why not nine-one-one?"

Maria raised her head. She looked pleadingly at me.

I sighed.

"It's better if you tell him, Maria,"
I said. "They're going to find out anyway."

"But if they do—" Maria shook her
head. "No."

"You can explain."

"Is there a problem?" Mr. Mason asked.

"Tell him, Maria."

Finally she admitted the truth: She was
in the country illegally and was afraid to
call the police.

"I see," Mr. Mason said. "Then what
happened?"

Maria stole a glance at me.

"I called Connie," she said. I held my
breath. "Then I left. When Connie came,
she called the police."

The last part was a lie, told to protect
me. I felt terrible deceiving Mr. Mason.
I promised myself I would explain later.

Mr. Mason leaned back in his chair.
"Is there anything else you want to tell me
about that morning, Maria?"

She shook her head.

"Did you touch anything?"

She shook her head again.

"The police found your fingerprints on the murder weapon," he said. "In the blood."

What? How was that possible?

"I picked up the statue," she said. "I wasn't thinking."

"You said you thought there was a burglar in the house," Mr. Mason said. "Did you hear someone or something that made you think that?"

"No. But how else could Mr. Richard have been killed? Who else would do such a thing?"

"Did you notice if anything was taken?"

"I didn't look," she admitted. "But in the bedroom, everything looked normal. Then, after I called Connie, I left."

Mr. Mason closed the leather portfolio in which he had been making notes. He tucked his pen into his jacket pocket.

"I'll find out when they plan to arraign you," he said.

I explained to her what that meant.

"Can he get me out of here?" Maria asked me. "Can I get bail?"

When I translated, Mr. Mason shook his head.

"They've charged you with murder, Maria. It's very hard to get bail on a murder charge. And once they know about your status..."

Maria began to cry. I didn't blame her. A murder conviction would mean prison, but deportation would mean certain death.

"I didn't kill Mr. Richard. I would never kill Mr. Richard," Maria said through her tears.

Mr. Mason told her to sit tight. I hugged her. Then we had to leave her alone in the cold, bare room.

# CHAPTER FIVE

Bodie's eyes zeroed in on me the moment I stepped out of the interview room. I ignored him as best I could.

"There's something I have to tell you," I said to Mr. Mason. "In private." I wanted to explain about when I had arrived and when Maria had left the house.

A cell phone trilled. He reached into his pocket and checked the display. "Sorry," he said. "I have to take this. We'll talk later. I promise." He walked away with his phone to his ear.

I turned to leave too. Bodie was blocking my way.

"Ms. Suarez, do you have a moment?" he asked. "I have a few more questions for you."

"I'm in a hurry," I said. I didn't want to speak to him again.

"You're not a suspect, if that's what you're worried about," he said. "Please?" He offered me a smile that made him look almost handsome. "It will just take a few minutes. We can sit in here."

He opened the door to a small room. I looked inside. It was just like the room Maria was in. An interview room. I felt myself bristle. Bodie noticed.

"Is there some reason you don't want to talk to me?" he asked.

"Are you trying to intimidate me, Detective?" I asked.

"Of course not. I'm just trying to get

all my facts straight. Look, I understand she's your friend."

"We work together. That's all."

"You're the person she called."

What was he getting at? He had told Mr. Mason I wasn't a suspect. Had he been lying?

I looked at my watch. "I don't have much time. And I don't like the room."

I was surprised when he led me to another room—the coffee room this time. We sat down.

"I understand from your employer that you were a legal assistant until recently," he said. "I understand you were downsized."

"That's right."

"That's quite a comedown," he said. "One day you're in some rich lawyer's office, the next day you're scrubbing toilets in some rich old man's house. Is that where you met Ms. Gonzales?"

I nodded.

"Did she ever speak to you about Mr. Withers?" he asked.

"We worked for him. Of course we talked about him."

"Did she ever mention him in a romantic context?"

"No."

"Did she ever say or do anything that made you think she might be romantically interested in him?"

"No." I knew that Maria liked the old man. She often said how sweet he was and what a gentleman he was. But romantically involved? No. I had been completely surprised by her announcement that the old man had proposed marriage.

"What about Mr. Withers?" Bodie asked.

"He was pleasant to both of us," I said. "I never noticed anything special between him and Ms. Gonzales."

Another detective called Bodie's name. "There's a guy here to see you," he said.

"Ask him to wait." Bodie shifted his eyes back to me.

"He's kind of antsy," the other detective said. "He said it's about his father—Richard Withers."

Bodie's eyes didn't move from my face. "Tell him I'll be with him in a minute."

The other detective vanished.

"I'd better let you go," I said, standing to leave.

"Just one more question, Ms. Suarez." Bodie stood up too. "Do you think Ms. Gonzales killed Mr. Withers?"

"No," I said. "What motive would she have for doing that?"

"Did you know about her status, Ms. Suarez?"

I remained silent. I wasn't being charged with anything. I wasn't under arrest. I didn't even have to talk to him if I didn't want to.

"Do you know that she claims Mr. Withers proposed to her?"

"Claims? Don't you believe her?" I asked.

He didn't answer. "Thank you for your time, Ms. Suarez. If anything comes up, I know where to find you."

He called for a uniformed officer to escort me to the main door. While I waited, I saw him approach a middle-aged man and introduce himself. He had to be Mr. Withers's son, I decided. Even from where I was standing, I saw the resemblance to his father and to the pictures of the young boy and the teenager that I had dusted throughout Mr. Withers's house. His face was pale and drawn. He was obviously in shock. My heart went out to him. How awful it must have been to find out that his father had been brutally murdered.

When I finally got outside, I saw that there was a message on my cell phone from Mike Czernecki. I returned his call.

"Do you have a job for me?" I asked.

47

"I'm working on it," he said. "I have a girl in the west end. She does nine houses. I've been getting complaints about her. I'm probably going to have to let her go."

"Nine houses?"

"Half day each on eight of them. Full day on the ninth. It's a good gig, Connie."

It was steady work, which would be good, sure. But nine different houses meant nine different homeowners with nine different sets of rules to remember.

"In the meantime," Mike continued, "Mr. Withers wants you to go back to the house."

Before I could remind him that Mr. Withers was dead, he said, "Mr. Withers junior, obviously. The son. His wife called me. She said she found the company name at her father-in-law's house. She says her husband wants the house cleaned from top to bottom. Walls and floors washed. Carpets shampooed. Fridge and cupboards

48

cleaned out. Closest contents sorted, boxed and labeled. It'll take you a week, minimum. Probably more like two. I told her you'd be there first thing in the morning. You good with that, Connie?"

I wasn't sure I wanted to go back there.

"Connie, is that a yes or a no? I don't have all day."

"Yes," I said. It was work, and I needed work. "About that other job—"

"When I let that girl go, you'll be the first to know. And I'm not going to hold it against you that you didn't tell me about Maria."

"I didn't know, Mike."

He snorted in reply. He still didn't believe me. But he knew I worked hard, and I was willing to bet no one had ever complained about me.

"Hey, Connie? If I were you, I wouldn't mention to either the son or the daughter-in-law that you know Maria. Maybe I wouldn't even mention that you've been in the house before. You hear what I'm saying?"

"Yes. Okay."

"And since they need so much done and they want it done fast, I negotiated a higher fee. You get twenty percent more on this one."

"Thanks, Mike," I said. That was how much I needed the work—and whatever else Mike could find for me.

But a twenty-percent increase on next to nothing was still next to nothing. It was like thanking a nobleman for scraps from his table.

# CHAPTER SIX

I recognized Mr. Withers's daughter-in-law Enid as soon as she opened the door. I had seen her at the house, usually snooping around Mr. Withers's study when he wasn't looking. But she didn't recognize me. She scanned me from head to toe but didn't stand aside to let me in.

"I'm the maid," I said. "From Missy Maids."

"ID," she demanded, her arms crossed in front of her designer sweater.

I dug out the laminated ID card that I hadn't had to show since my first day on the job. I held it out to her, but she refused to take it. Instead, she looked from the picture to my face—twice—to make sure I was who I said I was.

"Very well." She moved aside. "Follow me."

She led me up the stairs to the master bedroom. The police crime scene unit had gone over the room thoroughly. A big square of carpet had been cut out where Mr. Withers had been lying. There was fingerprint powder on most of the furniture, on the doorknobs and on the light switches.

"I want this room scrubbed from top to bottom," Enid Withers said. "No shortcuts. And never mind the carpet— obviously. Ten thousand dollars and it's completely ruined. Do you understand what you're supposed to do?"

I nodded.

"I'll be downstairs if you have any questions. But Mr. Czernecki told me that

you can manage without a lot of super-
vision. You can, can't you? If I have to stand
over you and tell you how to do everything,
I might as well do it myself."

"I can manage," I said.

"If you find anything and you don't
know where it belongs, leave it on the
dresser and I'll take care of it. Understand?"

"I understand perfectly," I said. I enjoyed
the look of surprise on her face. I was
willing to bet that she had expected a
thicker accent.

With that, she left me to my work.

* * *

I pulled on rubber gloves and set to work in
the bathroom. I scrubbed every surface until
it gleamed. I washed the floor. I polished the
massive mirror over the sink. As I did, I imagined Maria standing in front of it, fresh from
her shower and not yet knowing that her
world was about to be turned upside down.

After the bathroom, I moved into the bedroom. I wiped and polished all the furniture. I straightened the things on the dresser—the silver brushes, the little scissors, several bottles of cologne. I remembered the scent that had lingered when I had found Mr. Withers's body. I remembered the first time he had gone overboard with his cologne. I had developed a full-blown allergy attack. He had never used it again while I was in the house. But he'd obviously put some on for Maria. I stripped and remade the bed, and vacuumed the carpet. I was putting my supplies back into my tray and getting ready to move on to the next room when Enid appeared. She scanned the room.

"Did you clean everywhere?" she demanded.

I nodded.

"Under the bed?" she asked.

I nodded again.

"Under all the furniture?"

"Yes," I said.

"Did you find anything?"

"No," I said.

"Are you sure?"

"I'm sure," I said. Did she think I had taken something? Is that why she was asking? "Would you like me to start on the other bedrooms?"

Before she could answer, the doorbell rang. I expected her to tell me to answer it, but she didn't. She hurried to get it herself. I followed her as far as the top of the stairs to wait for her instructions.

"Is Mr. Withers here?" a man's voice asked.

"Mr. Withers is deceased," Enid said.

"Mr. Charles Withers," the man clarified.

"I'm afraid—oh, there's his car now." I heard a car pull up to the side of the house. A moment later someone entered through the mudroom door and walked through the kitchen.

"Charles," Enid called, "there's someone here to see you."

Though I couldn't see him, Mr. Withers obviously stepped into the hallway.

"Albert Camden," the man said. "I'm your father's attorney, Mr. Withers."

"Ah, yes," Charles said. He sounded breathless. "Please come in. Is this about the will?"

"Yes." There was a slight pause before Mr. Camden said, "Madam, I don't believe we've been introduced."

"This is my wife," Charles said.

"My pleasure," Mr. Camden said smoothly. "Mr. Withers, I don't know if you are aware of it, but your father recently made a new will."

"New will?" Charles and Enid said, almost in unison.

"Normally I would have had my assistant call to arrange a meeting in my office with all interested parties," Mr. Camden continued. "But it came to my attention that you were having the house cleaned in anticipation of…well, I believe you intended to take possession of it."

"How did that *come to your attention*?" Enid asked.

"*Intended* to take possession?" Charles asked.

"Who told you about our intentions?" Enid demanded.

"There are accounts to be settled," Mr. Camden said, ignoring her angry tone. "My assistant contacted Mr. Withers's regular suppliers to ask about any outstanding invoices. One was for a maid service. That is how I found out that a maid had been hired to clean the house and that the bill for her services is to be added to the month's bill."

"Is there a problem with that?" Charles asked.

"As a matter of fact, yes," Mr. Camden said.

"What problem?" Enid asked.

"Perhaps we could sit down for a moment and I could explain—"

"Perhaps you could just get to the point," Enid said.

There was a moment's silence, and I imagined Mr. Camden studying the couple before continuing.

"Quite simply," he said at last, "you, Mr. Withers, do not have the authority to add any expenses to the accounts of your father's estate. Nor do you have the right to take possession of this house. Mr. Withers left it to his fiancée."

"You can't be serious," Charles said. "She's a *maid*."

"I'm very serious," Mr. Camden said. "Mr. Withers changed his will to leave this house and certain other assets to her."

"What other assets?" Enid demanded.

"Ms. Gonzales *murdered* my father," Charles said. "Surely that means she can't inherit from him."

"That charge has yet to be proven—beyond a reasonable doubt, as they say. And then there's the matter of any child that might result from the union."

"Child?" Enid said. "He included provisions for a child?"

"*Might* result?" Charles was almost shouting. "He's dead. He was murdered. How can anything result?"

"Nevertheless," Mr. Camden said, "I'm afraid I'm going to have to ask you to vacate the premises until the matter is settled."

"I'll challenge the will," Charles said, interrupting him. "Anyone can see what happened. That woman threw herself at my father. She tricked him into changing his will. Then, when she got what she wanted, she killed him."

"If you want to challenge the will, you are free to do so," Mr. Camden said. "In the meantime, I have to ask you to vacate the premises and surrender the keys."

"I don't believe this!" Enid growled. "Charles, do something!"

"I'll take care of it," Charles said. I heard the faint jingle of keys and then the sharp sound of metal being slapped onto a table. "There," he said. "There's my key."

"And you, Mrs. Withers?" Mr. Camden said. "Do *you* have a key?"

"Give it to him, Enid," Charles said.

Enid's voice was bitter. "You'll be hearing from *our* lawyer."

I heard footsteps, then silence.

Suddenly I was afraid that everyone had gone.

"Wait!" I called.

A man came to the bottom of the stairs and looked up at me. Mr. Camden.

"I'm the maid," I said. "Just let me get my things."

I ran back to the bedroom and retrieved my tray. Mr. Camden waited for me and, like a true gentleman, held the door.

\* \* \*

Mike called after I got home.

"You have to talk louder," I said. The workmen were making progress. At this rate, they would be working in my apartment the next day.

"I have a request for you," Mike said, shouting into the phone.

"You mean another job?"

"Not exactly. Not yet, anyway," he said. "But I'm working on it."

"Then what?"

"Some people want to talk to you. The old man's son and daughter-in-law."

"The Witherses want to talk to *me*? What about?"

"She didn't say."

"She?" I asked.

"The wife. She says she wants to talk to the maid who found the old man's body. She says it's important. She wanted me to give her your name and address so she could see you right away."

"You didn't give it to her, did you?"

"No," Mike said. "You know my policy."

I did. Mike believed in confidentiality—for both his clients and his employees. I was grateful.

"But I told her that I would give you the message and tell you that she's expecting you at her house at six o'clock tomorrow evening. You got a pen?"

"I didn't say yes, Mike."

I imagined Enid Withers demanding my presence instead of asking for it. I also imagined the look of shock on her face when she found out that the maid whose presence she was demanding had been under her nose all morning.

"But you will go, right, Connie?"

"I don't know." It was the truth. Part of me wanted to say no simply because I didn't like Charles and Enid Withers. But the rest of me was curious about what they wanted. "Why do you even care, Mike?" I asked. "They aren't clients of yours."

"They are since they hired you to clean the old man's house," Mike said. "I told the wife what your situation is— that you're out of work. So she came up with a job for you for tomorrow. She wants the condo of a friend cleaned before the friend returns from Europe. She's willing to pay you well. You put in the day there, make some money, and then go and talk to her and her husband. Sounds good, right?"

"How well is she willing to pay?"

"Three times your regular rate."

"That sounds like a bribe, Mike," I said. "What does she want from me?"

"Probably information about Maria and the old man. That's another thing you didn't tell me about, Connie—that Maria was planning to marry Withers. I'm doing you a favor. Take the money. You need it. Talk to them. If you don't want to do it for yourself, do it for the company."

"The company?"

"Those people live in a great neighborhood," Mike said. "A neighborhood where the women have high-powered jobs—*if* they work. Either way, they don't do their own housework. If we do the Witherses a favor, maybe they'll do us a favor—get us some referrals."

"*Us*? Don't you mean you, Mike?" I said. "And do you really think they're going to recommend Missy Maids after this?"

"You never know. Besides, I've got nothing to lose here," Mike said. "Neither do you."

"What's in it for me?" I asked. "Besides the triple pay?"

Mike snorted. "You're starting to sound like me. What's in it for you is I get on the phone right now and fire that other girl and you get a brand-new roster of clients."

I may have sounded like him, but I wasn't at all like him. I didn't want to profit from someone else's misfortune.

"Get me a different roster," I said. "New people. Full days. No half days."

"Connie, if I could, I would—"

"That's the deal, Mike. If you don't have any houses, get me some offices. I know you can do it." Mike had cousins in the office-cleaning business. He could get me something if he wanted to. "If you give me what I want, I'll give you what you want."

There was a long pause. I fought the urge to take back everything I had just said. What if he told me to forget it? What if I'd just thrown away the only work I had?

"Okay," he said finally. "I'll see what I can do."

That was a yes. Otherwise he would have fired me outright.

"Call me when you have something definite. Then I'll call the Witherses."

When the phone rang half an hour later, I thought it was Mike.

It wasn't.

It was Maria.

# CHAPTER SEVEN

"Where are you, Maria?" I asked.

"They moved me. It's a place for women. Mr. Mason says they'll make me stay here until the trial."

"Are you okay?"

"They insult me so much, Connie. Mr. Mason was here. He told me Mr. Richard's son and daughter-in-law got the police to search my apartment. And they demanded to know everything I had with me when they arrested me. They say they know I stole from Mr. Richard. But you know what? They didn't find anything. I'm not a thief."

I didn't know what to say.

"And, Connie, he also told me about Mr. Richard's will. He says Mr. Richard left almost everything to me."

"I heard," I said. "But I don't think you should talk about it on the phone, Maria. I can't see you tomorrow, but I'll come the next day. I promise."

"Mr. Richard was a nice man. He said someone like me who works so hard deserves to have something good happen. But he never said anything about his will, Connie. He just asked me to marry him. I think he was lonely all alone in that big house. I think he wanted someone to look after him. I told him I love to do that. Also I could help my family, send them more money, maybe bring them up here. But I never expected him to die and leave me so much."

"We can talk when I see you," I said again. "Not over the phone."

"Sure," she said. "But Connie, you're a lawyer. When they let me out of here—"

Hadn't she heard Mr. Mason? There was no way she would get bail.

"—they'll deport me for sure. What do you think? Can I can still inherit from him even if I live in another country?"

If I was right about what would happen to her when she was deported, she wouldn't have time to worry about inheriting.

"Maria, we really shouldn't—"

"Just tell me, Connie."

"Yes, you can inherit," I said. "If it's a valid will. And if his son doesn't contest it."

"Contest it?"

"Go to court to challenge it," I explained.

"How can he do that? It's up to Mr. Richard what he wants to do with his money."

"Yes and no," I said. "His son could argue that his father didn't know what he was doing when he made the new will.

Or that you manipulated him into changing it and then killed him to get the money."

"I would never do such a thing!" She sounded shocked.

"It's not a good idea to talk about it on the phone, Maria."

"I would never kill Mr. Richard. I would never kill anyone. I would never manipulate anyone either."

I wondered about that. I'd thought I knew Maria. I felt sorry for her situation. But obviously I didn't know her as well as I thought. I'd had no idea that she had asked for rich male clients. She hadn't told me that she had quit Mike's agency and that Mr. Withers was paying her directly. Or that she was sleeping with Mr. Withers. I wondered if she really was surprised to find she'd been in his will.

"I'll come and see you the day after tomorrow, Maria," I said. "We can talk then."

* * *

I spent the next day scrubbing the huge penthouse apartment that belonged to Enid Withers's friend. Some bribe, I thought. I had to work hard to earn it. When I finally finished, it was time to pay the Witherses a visit.

Nobody—neither Mike nor Enid Withers—warned me about the roadwork that was being done near the entrance to the subdivision where Charles and Enid Withers lived. I had to sit in a line of traffic for a full ten minutes before it was my turn to pass.

The subdivision was relatively new. It was filled with large houses, landscaped properties and late-model cars. Charles and Enid obviously weren't hurting for money. But their house wasn't nearly as magnificent as Richard Withers's house. The son had done well for himself, but not as well as the father.

Enid answered the door. She looked confused when she saw me. Mike obviously hadn't explained to her who I was. I had to do it myself. To be polite, I also thanked her for the day's work at her friend's condo.

"Come in," she said. She didn't even try to be welcoming. "Charles!"

Charles Withers appeared from the back of the house. As he stood beside his wife, I noticed that she looked at least ten years older than him.

"You must be Connie," he said. His smile reminded me of his father's. "I hope you didn't get too tied up in all that roadwork. There's a shortcut you can use. I'll give you directions before you leave."

"Thank you," I said.

Soft music was playing in the background. I smelled fresh coffee, as well as perfume and cologne. The perfume was strong and overpowering. The cologne was soft and mellow. They both had an immediate reaction on me. I felt my sinuses start to close and my head start to ache.

"Please come in," Charles said.

I stayed where I was.

"Your perfume and cologne are really strong. Would you mind washing them off?" I held up my wrist to show him my MedicAlert bracelet.

Enid's mouth twisted down, as if she couldn't believe what I was asking.

"I'm sorry, but I really can't come in if you smell like that," I said. I didn't care if she thought I was being rude.

"Of course," Charles said. "Of course."

Enid scowled. Charles looked pleadingly at her. They left me standing at the door while they disappeared. I heard their voices—hers furious, his soothing. When they came back, the only aroma I detected was the faint scent of soap. It would fade fast.

"Thank you," I said.

Charles started to lead me into the living room. Enid stopped him.

"I'm sure Ms. Suarez would be more comfortable in the kitchen," she said. "I made coffee."

Charles opened his mouth to say something. Maybe he was thinking the same thing I was: Why did she think I would be more comfortable in the kitchen? Because I was a maid? Because my name was Suarez?

"This way," Enid said, her voice insistent. Charles's mouth closed and he trotted after her. I followed.

The kitchen was large and bright and looked out through a wall of windows to a backyard patio and garden.

"Please sit," Enid directed.

I did as I was told. She set a cup of coffee in front of me without asking if I wanted it. She and Charles waited until I had added a little milk before Charles said, "You're probably wondering why we asked you here."

"I am," I admitted.

"I understand you worked for my father for the past six months. You and Ms. Gonzales."

"That's right. I'm very sorry for your loss, Mr. Withers," I said. "Your father was a good man. And an interesting one."

"How would you know that?" Enid demanded.

"He liked to talk," I said. "He was curious about my country. And Maria's. He asked us a lot of questions, and I think he must have started reading about them because—"

"Charles, get to the point," Enid said, cutting me off. "Ask her."

I looked at Charles.

"Ask me what?" I asked.

"I don't know if you're aware of it, Ms. Suarez, but Ms. Gonzales claims that my father intended to marry her."

"Of course she's aware," Enid said.

"My father was eighty-three years old," Charles said.

"Really?" I was surprised. Mr. Withers had told us he was seventy-one. I wondered if Maria knew his real age. If she didn't, had he lied to make himself more attractive to her? "He was very fit for his age."

"What's that supposed to mean?" Enid demanded.

Charles sighed. "Enid, please." Enid slouched in her chair like a resentful teenager. "My father may have seemed fit, but he was old and sometimes forgetful—"

"—and confused," Enid added quickly. "He was always losing things."

"Who was always losing things?" a voice behind me asked. Enid jumped.

I turned and saw a tall, lean man in jeans and a snug T-shirt. He was handsome, with sandy hair and green eyes and a smooth, tanned body. He dropped a small suitcase onto the tiled floor.

"Andrew, when did you get back?"

"Aren't you glad to see me, Mother?" he asked. He dropped a kiss onto her cheek.

"My stepson," Charles explained to me. Enid gave him a sharp look.

"Our *son*," she corrected.

Andrew smiled at me.

"Aren't you going to introduce me, Mother?" he asked.

"Ms. Suarez—" Charles began.

"—is a maid who worked for your grandfather," Enid said.

"Really?" Andrew said, his eyes still on me. I felt myself blush. "Lucky Grandpa. He sure knows how to live."

"Didn't you tell him?" Charles asked.

"Tell me what?" Andrew said.

"About what happened to my father. He—"

"It can wait," Enid said. "Andrew, your father and I need to talk with Ms. Suarez. Why don't you go and unpack. We'll talk later."

"Yes, Mother," he said with a wry smile. He kissed her on the cheek again and left the kitchen.

"I'll be plain, Ms. Suarez," Enid said once he was gone. "My father-in-law was a forgetful old man who should not have been living alone."

I had suspected why she had asked me here. Now I knew I was right.

"He seemed fine to me," I said. "He read a lot. He listened to music. He liked to talk about his books and music. He didn't seem at all forgetful."

"To you and Ms. Gonzales," she said, her tone making it clear that she didn't believe me.

"Yes," I said. "I spoke to him almost every day. Is this about the will, Mrs. Withers?"

"What do you know about that?" Enid asked.

"I know he left a lot of money and property to Maria Gonzales. If you want me to say that Mr. Withers wasn't thinking straight when he made that will, I'm afraid I can't help you."

Enid leaned back in her chair and folded her arms over her chest. "Were you in on it with Ms. Gonzales? Did she promise you something in exchange for helping her to pressure that poor old man into cutting his own son out of his will?"

I stood up.

"Whatever happened between Mr. Withers and Ms. Gonzales is their business, not mine," I said.

Charles jumped to his feet.

"My wife didn't mean to insult you, Ms. Suarez," he said. "It's just—" He sighed. "As I'm sure you can imagine, it was quite a shock to discover that my father had changed his will and left everything to a woman he barely knows."

"Love is sometimes difficult to explain, Mr. Withers," I said. "Men have done stranger and more foolish things."

"So you agree it was foolish?" Enid said.

"I didn't mean—"

"Especially when they weren't married yet," she said, cutting me off. "Especially when there was every chance that he would eventually see that little tramp for what she really was."

"Enid, please—"

"Oh, he was smitten with your little friend," Enid continued, ignoring her husband. "But he was a successful man. He got rich by his wits and hard work. Do you know that Ms. Gonzales has a boyfriend and a child back home in Honduras?"

"Honduras?" What was she talking about? "Maria is from Colombia."

"Originally," Enid said. "But she was living in Honduras before she came here. That's where she left her child."

"I don't believe it," I said. But what if I was wrong? What if this was one more thing Maria hadn't told me?

"It's true," Enid said. "I knew it and Richard knew it. He's no fool. He obviously had her investigated."

"How do you know that?" Charles asked her.

"I saw the report the last time I was there."

I remembered seeing her in Mr. Withers's study. "You snooped," I said.

"The police didn't mention any of this," Charles said.

"That's because that little tart probably destroyed the report after she killed your father," Enid said. "And I bet he didn't find out the truth about that little gold digger until after she got him to change his will. I bet he called off the wedding, and that's why she killed him."

"Did you tell the police?" Charles asked.

"Of course I did," she snapped. "But the report is missing and there's no indication of who prepared it."

I stood up. My head was spinning. Was this true? Had the old man discovered the truth about Maria? Had he called off the wedding? Had Maria—?

"I should go," I said.

"Do you like being a maid, Ms. Suarez?" Enid asked.

"I beg your pardon?"

"You heard me. Do you like being a maid?"

"Enid—" Charles began.

She waved a hand to silence him.

"My father-in-law was a wealthy man," she said, her eyes drilling into mine. "I am sure that he would have wanted to compensate you for your loyalty. That can be arranged."

I looked evenly at her.

"Are you trying to bribe me, Mrs. Withers?"

"I am just pointing out what we would be able to do for you if my father-in-law's will were carried out as he intended."

"In other words, you'll pay me if I tell the police that Maria coerced Mr. Withers into changing his will," I said.

She smiled thinly. "Your English really is excellent," she said.

"I am not going to ask how much you are prepared to pay me, Mrs. Withers," I said. "Because if I asked you that and you answered, that would be a bribe to get me to lie to the police. And I would have to report it. I don't know anything about what went on between Maria and your father-in-law. All I know is what I saw with my own eyes, which is that she made him laugh and that he treated her with dignity."

With that, I let myself out of the kitchen and out of their house. I was shaking with rage—at Enid and at Maria. I glanced in the rearview mirror as I drove away. Enid was watching me from the open door.

# CHAPTER EIGHT

All I wanted was to get home. But I got stuck in traffic again. The road crew was long gone, but there was only one lane open. Cars were taking turns passing, first in one direction and then the other. I wished I had asked for directions to the shortcut Charles had mentioned.

It was dark and I was tired by the time I pulled into the parking lot behind the building where I lived. Most of the lights in the parking lot were burned out and had been for months. Usually I tried to park near the road where there was light from the streetlamps. But tonight there were no spaces. I had to park way over to one side near an empty building that had been for sale for months. It was dark over there.

I locked my car and had just started across the dreary lot when someone or something slammed into me from behind. When I tried to turn, something hit me hard in the face. What was going on? Was I going to be sexually assaulted? Was I going to die here in this parking lot? I felt my purse being ripped from my shoulder. I opened my mouth to scream. A fist hammered into my belly. I sank to my knees, gasping for air and clinging to the strap of my purse. My attacker punched me again. I refused to let go of my purse. I clung to it with one hand and grabbed my attacker's gloved hand with the other.

Suddenly I heard ferocious barking. A massive black animal shot toward me. I heard a grunt of surprise and fell backward, holding an empty glove as my attacker ran.

"Brutus! Brutus, stay!" a voice yelled from across the parking lot.

Brutus was an enormous black rottweiler who lived with his owner down the hall from me. He continued to bark and growl.

"Brutus!"

Tony Milano, Brutus's owner, appeared, a chain leash dangling from one hand. He peered into the darkness for a moment before reaching down and helping me to my feet.

"Are you okay, Connie?" he asked.

My head was throbbing and my stomach hurt. But I nodded.

"I've complained to the management company a dozen times about those burned-out lights," he said. "They never listen." He snapped the leash onto Brutus's collar. "Maybe now they'll have to."

I stared at the large leather glove in my hand.

"I'm glad you came along when you did—you *and* Brutus. He almost got away with my purse."

"He's a coward, if you ask me. Lurking in the darkness to attack a woman. And you know what else? The little twerp runs like a girl." He stared into the darkness with a look of disgust on his face. "You want to call the cops? I doubt they'll be able to do anything, but if we have a police report, it might help to pressure the building management to fix the lights."

I said okay. As I suspected, the police weren't about to send a squad car for what sounded to them like an attempted purse snatching. I had to go to the police station to file a report. Tony gave me a lift and drove me home afterward. He and Brutus walked me to my apartment door. I was grateful. I lived at the back of the second floor, right next to the stairwell. Tony pulled a business card from his pocket.

"If you get nervous in the next couple of days and want someone to walk you to your car, call me," he said. "I mean it, Connie."

As I thanked him, I noticed how blue his eyes were. I had never seen them this close up. I went inside and double-locked the door.

\* \* \*

I planned to sleep in the next morning, but someone hammered on my door bright and early. It was the work crew. They had finally made it to my apartment. No sooner had I let them in than the phone rang.

It was Maria.

"You're coming to see me today, Connie, *sí*?" she asked.

"*Sí*, Maria."

"Can you bring my Bible?"

"Sure. Where is it?"

"In my dresser. In the top drawer. And, Connie, if you could bring me some soap—"

Somewhere on the other end of the line, someone yelled.

"Is everything okay, Maria?"

"There's always a line for the phone," she said. "Ask Luisa to let you in. You remember her. She lives across the hall." Her voice dropped to a whisper. "Some of the women in here, they scare me."

"Maria—"

But the phone was already dead.

I got dressed. The side of my face was bruised and swollen where I had been hit. I covered the mark with makeup as best as I could and made myself something to eat. I dug out the keys that I had picked up off Mr. Withers's floor and headed for the elevator, leaving the workmen to start on my apartment.

My knees trembled when I crossed the parking lot, even though it was morning.

I couldn't help thinking what might have happened if Brutus and Tony hadn't come to my rescue.

I drove to the building where Maria lived. The place was shabby compared to my building. The security door was unlocked, and the lobby smelled of stale cigarettes, urine and vomit. No wonder Maria wanted to work for rich people.

Two of the four elevators were out of order and one seemed permanently stalled in the basement, so I walked the seven floors up to Maria's apartment. The stairwell smelled worse than the lobby.

Maria had told me her neighbor Luisa would let me in, but I didn't see any reason to bother her when I had Maria's keys in my purse. I dug them out. There were three keys on the ring. I slipped what I assumed was the apartment key into the lock. It wouldn't turn. I pulled it out again and selected another key. Just then the door across the hall opened and a head popped out.

"*Hola*, Connie."

"*Hola*, Luisa," I said. The second key didn't fit either.

"How is Maria?"

I told her what I knew.

"The police came," Luisa said. "They searched the whole apartment. It took me forever to straighten everything up after they left."

I slipped the third and last key into the keyhole. It didn't turn either.

"This place is worse than mine," I muttered. "At least my keys work."

"Our keys work," Luisa said indignantly. "The property managers installed new locks only last week. You must have the old ones."

She disappeared into her apartment and was back a moment later with a single key on a string. "Maria and I have copies of each other's keys, just in case." She slipped it into the lock, turned it easily and pushed open the door.

I dropped the useless keys onto Maria's tiny coffee table and got some soap from the bathroom. I found the Bible in the bedroom. When I picked it up, something slipped out from between the pages. A photograph. I picked it up and looked at it. The photo was of Maria with a handsome young man. The young man had his arm around her.

It was Andrew Withers.

# CHAPTER NINE

The guard at the detention center searched me and my purse. He searched the Bible too, leafing through the pages and holding it up by the spine to see if anything fell out. Finally he said, "It will be given to the inmate."

I met with Maria in a long room that was divided in half by a wall of Plexiglas. Tables lined both sides of the wall. Between each table was a divider that offered only the smallest amount of privacy. Attached to each divider was a phone. I sat at the table

I had been assigned. Maria appeared through a door on the other side. She smiled when she saw me.

"You brought my Bible?" she asked as soon as she picked up the phone on her side of the glass.

"I had to leave it with the guard. He said he would give it to you."

She nodded.

"Maria, I found a picture," I said. "Of you and Mr. Withers's grandson."

She frowned. "His grandson? I don't know Mr. Richard's grandson. Where did you find this picture, Connie?"

"In your Bible. He has his arm around you."

Recognition flickered in her eyes.

"You mean Andrew," she said.

"Yes. Andrew Withers."

"His name is Andrew Stevenson," Maria said.

"Maybe that's the name he gave you—"

"I saw it on his driver's license."

I remembered what Charles had said when Enid introduced Andrew to me. Maybe Charles hadn't formally adopted Andrew. Or maybe Andrew had decided to keep his own name.

"Were you seeing him, Maria?" I asked.

"We went out a few times. But it was nothing."

"How did you meet him?"

"I was in the park, and he came up to me. He's very nice, but…" She shrugged.

"Not rich enough?" I asked.

She smiled. "No, not rich enough. But he helped me get the job at Mr. Richard's."

"He did?"

"I told him I was working for Mike, and he told me he knew someone who was always looking for some help. The next thing I knew, Mike sent me to this man's house, the one Andrew knew. That's how I started working there."

"Mike never told me that." In fact, Mike had made it seem as if *he* was the one who had found the job.

"Mike likes to take credit for everything," Maria said. "I was grateful to Andrew. But I didn't want to go out with him."

"When was the last time you saw him?"

"A few months ago. I kept telling him I wasn't interested."

"*Kept* telling him?"

"He called me. He showed up at my apartment. I told him he had to stop doing that."

"Did you tell him you were in love with Mr. Withers?"

"How could I?" Maria said. "I didn't know myself until a few weeks ago."

And as of yesterday, Andrew hadn't known that Mr. Withers was dead. He had been away somewhere.

"What about your boyfriend and your child back home, Maria?"

She sat up straight. "How do you know about them?"

"Enid Withers told me," I said. "Mr. Withers knew about them, didn't he?"

She hung her head. "Yes," she said softly.

"Did you tell him or did he tell you?"

She was silent for a moment. When she raised her head, her eyes were filled with tears.

"He asked me if there was any reason I couldn't marry him," she said quietly. "At first I didn't know what he was talking about. Then I saw something in his eyes. He had papers—information about me. I was so ashamed for lying. So I told him everything. I said I was sorry. I said I love my daughter, but I don't love her father. I also said I understood if he didn't want me because of her. Do you know what he said, Connie?"

I shook my head.

"He said he loved me no matter what. He said he wanted to marry me and make me happy. He said he wanted my daughter to feel like a princess and that he couldn't wait to meet her. Then he tore up the papers he had about me and threw them away."

"You told me you were on the run from Colombian gangsters, Maria. You didn't tell me you lived in Honduras."

"I had to leave Colombia. I went to Honduras first, and then I came here."

She had an answer for everything. I didn't know whether to believe her or not.

"Tell me everything about that morning."

"I *have* told you everything, Connie."

"Tell me again."

Slowly she went through the events of the morning Mr. Withers had been murdered. When she finished, I asked, "What about any smells?"

"What do you mean?"

"I smelled something when I got there. Cologne, I think. Did you notice it?"

She shook her head.

"Are you sure?"

"I'm sure."

"Was Mr. Withers wearing cologne that morning?"

A smile crossed her face.

"He liked to smell nice," she said. "Sometimes he put on too much, and it made me sneeze. Then we both laughed."

"Did his cologne have vanilla tones?"

"I don't know," Maria said. "You smell things that I don't even notice, Connie. He just wears something nice. That's all I know."

A guard appeared and told Maria her time was up. Maria had one last question for me.

"Connie, do you think they will let me go? I don't want my baby to be born in a prison."

# CHAPTER TEN

I stared through the glass at Maria. Baby? She was pregnant?

"They have to let me out of here," she said before she was led away. "They have to let me get the money Mr. Richard left for me. I need it. The baby will need it."

"Did you tell the police about the baby, Maria?"

"No. The only person who knew was Mr. Richard."

* * *

After I left the detention center, I sat in my car and thought about Maria and Mr. Withers—and the baby. I was sure it was going to make things worse for Maria. Enid and Charles would claim that she got herself pregnant in order to coerce Mr. Withers into marriage and changing his will. That, together with Mike's testimony that she had requested only rich male clients, would make it seem as if she had planned something like this all along. Maria's baby would not be brought up in prison—but it wouldn't be brought up by Maria either.

Finally, I pulled out my phone and called Emma. She listened without interrupting, then gave me the phone number that I asked for.

* * *

Mr. Camden was frowning when he got out of his car a few hours later.

"I'm still not sure what it is you're after, Ms. Suarez," he said.

I explained to him about my allergies.

"I don't see what that has to do with Mr. Withers's estate," he said.

I explained that too, as best as I could.

He hunted in his pocket and pulled out a key.

"Okay," he said. "I'll give you five minutes, but I'm staying with you the whole time."

"Actually, I was going to ask you to come along," I said. I dug in my purse for my inhaler. "If I have an extreme reaction, I may need help."

He stepped back a half pace, his hands raised in protest.

"I'm not a doctor," he said.

"If I pass out—which I hope I won't— just call nine-one-one," I said.

"Maybe this isn't a good idea, Ms. Suarez," he said.

"Please, Mr. Camden. All I'm asking for is five minutes."

Reluctantly he agreed. He unlocked the front door and followed me up the stairs to Mr. Withers's bedroom. He hovered nervously behind me as I opened various bottles and containers and sniffed what was inside. He tensed up when I had to use the inhaler. He rushed to my side when I started to wheeze despite it. He didn't relax until we were outside again.

"Well?" he said. "Did you find what you were looking for?"

I shook my head.

"Now what?"

"Now I have to do a little more research. Then I guess I contact the police." But no matter how hard I tried, I couldn't imagine Bodie taking me seriously. Especially once he found out that Maria was pregnant—if he didn't already know.

* * *

Armed with a brand-new inhaler, I ventured into the main floor of the city's largest department store. Usually I avoided places like that. The main floor is always crowded with cosmetics counters with attractive young women in front of each of them, handing out scent cards and offering perfume samples. For me, this was usually a recipe for disaster.

But this time I braced myself. I held my breath as I marched past the cosmetics counters and headed for the back of the store where the masculine fragrances were displayed. There were so many of them.

"Can I help you?" asked an immaculately groomed young woman.

"Yes. I'm looking for a cologne," I said. "Something with a musky scent."

She smiled. "Almost everything we have has a musky scent."

"This has a hint of vanilla, I think."

She thought for a moment before pulling down seven or eight different bottles.

"These all have vanilla undertones," she said.

I pulled my inhaler out of my purse and set it onto the counter. Then I reached for the first bottle.

The woman blocked my hand.

"You have allergies," she said. It wasn't a question.

I nodded.

"You should stay away from this department," she said. "You should stay away from this whole floor." When I looked surprised, she said, "My sister has the same allergies. Once she had so much trouble breathing that she almost died."

"So I guess you know something about first aid?" I said.

She nodded. "But that doesn't mean I want to have to use it."

"This is important," I said.

"Trust me, there isn't a man on the planet who's worth it," she said.

"I still need to try," I said.

She studied me for a few seconds before pulling out a cell phone. "Just in case," she said. "I sure hope you know what you're doing.

* * *

I was never so glad to get out of a store and into the fresh air. My head was throbbing. My throat was constricted. I'd had to use the inhaler several times, and I was still having trouble breathing. If I had stayed in there for another minute, I don't know what would have happened.

But at least I had an answer.

I stood outside the store, gulping in the spring air. I didn't care that it smelled like exhaust fumes from all the cars that were circling around, looking for a parking space.

It was air—outside air—and that was all I cared about.

Before I headed back to my car, I called Bodie. I ended up in voice mail and, after the beep, left him a detailed message.

* * *

It was dark when I arrived back at my apartment building. Again all the parking spots near the road were gone. The overhead lights hadn't been fixed either. I felt my hand tremble as I got out of the car, peering around cautiously to make sure that no one was going to jump out at me. When I reached the edge of the darkness and stepped into where the lights were, I felt the tension leave my shoulders.

A dog barked.

Brutus.

He was pulling so hard on his leash that he had yanked Tony Milano's arm straight out in front of him.

"I see your bruise has faded," he said when he was close enough.

I nodded.

Brutus pulled harder at his leash.

"I think he's trying to tell you something," I said.

Tony laughed. As he trotted after Brutus, he turned back to me. "I hear your mother stopped by."

My mother? The last I had heard, my mother was in Mexico. I wanted to ask him what he meant, but he was already across the street.

My apartment reeked of glue from the new floors in the kitchen and bathroom and from the new countertops. I felt my throat closing up. I wasn't sure I could sleep here tonight. Maybe I could spend the night at Maria's. I was pretty sure Luisa would let me in if I explained my problem.

I put down my purse and reached for the light switch. Before I could flip it on, something flew out of the darkness at me. I crashed to the ground. What was happening? Who was it? Someone—a man—fell on top of me and pressed a rough hand over my mouth and nose. I fought back, bucking to get him off me. I kicked. I tried to bite his hand. Then I raised my knee, hard. He let out a groan and fell to the floor beside me. In a sliver of light from my kitchen window, I saw his face.

It was Charles Withers.

I started to get to my feet.

Something hit me from behind.

My knees buckled. I felt myself slide to the floor.

Blackness engulfed me.

# CHAPTER ELEVEN

I heard voices. Angry, hushed voices. Charles Withers's voice.

And Enid's.

"You said we wouldn't hurt her. You said—"

"She's fine," Enid said.

"But—"

"Why don't you wait outside, Charles? I'll let you know if I need you."

"They're not here, Enid. She doesn't have them. Let's get out of here."

I opened my eyes. All of the kitchen drawers and cupboards were open. My desk had been ransacked. The contents of my purse were strewn all over the kitchen table.

"What are you doing here? What do you want?" I asked. My face felt huge and swollen, like someone had stuffed my head with cotton.

Enid spun around. Something blinded me. A flashlight. It shone in my face and then snapped off.

"Oh my God," Charles said. "She's seen us. She'll call the police. She'll have us arrested. We broke into her apartment. We assaulted her."

"We didn't break in," Enid said. "Those workmen let me in."

I remembered what Tony had said outside about my mother stopping by. Now it made sense.

"You entered my apartment under false pretenses," I said. "That's illegal."

I thought about the attempt to grab me in the parking lot—and about Enid's instructions to me when I had gone to clean Mr. Withers's house after his murder. I also remembered what Maria had told me about her apartment being searched and about Charles and Enid wanting to know what she had on her when she was arrested. It was all adding up.

"And you assaulted me," I said. "Twice."

Light from the window washed Charles's face.

"Twice?" he said.

"Once just now. And once the night before last, in the parking lot."

"That's ridiculous," Charles said. "And we can explain—"

"You dropped a glove, Enid," I said. It was a man's glove, but I remembered how easily it had slipped off her hand. I also remembered what Tony had said: *He runs like a girl.* "The police have it. I gave it to them when I reported the assault. It's evidence."

Enid's whole body stiffened.

"What's she talking about, Enid?" Charles said. "What have you done? What have *we* done?"

"Nothing," Enid snapped. "Wait outside, Charles."

"You're looking for something," I said. But what? That's when it hit me. "It's the keys, isn't it?" That's why they hadn't worked in Maria's lock. "You told the police Maria stole from your father-in-law. You had her and her apartment searched. Did you tell them one of the things she took was a set of keys? The ones you left at your father's house after you killed him?"

"*We* didn't kill him," Charles said. He sounded horrified at the thought.

"But you *are* here for the keys, aren't you?"

"Enid left them at the house by mistake. She doesn't want the police to think—"

"That *she* killed him?" I said. I turned to her. "The keys were in his bedroom. That's where he was killed."

"We had nothing to do with that," Enid said. "We don't want any complications about the will, that's all. If the police think I was there, it might confuse the jury."

"You mean they might think that someone besides Maria killed Mr. Withers?" I said.

Charles was staring at his wife.

"You didn't tell me you dropped your keys in the bedroom," he said.

"What difference does it make? I didn't kill him," Enid said. "Why would I?"

"Because you found out he was going to marry Maria," I said. "So you killed him before he could do it and change his will. You didn't know that he'd already made a new one."

Enid was silent.

"Then you attacked me and tried to steal my purse. You were looking for your keys," I continued. "Now what are you going to do? Are you going to kill me too?"

"No!" Charles cried. "Nobody is going to kill anyone."

I didn't look at him. My eyes were locked on Enid.

"You know the police are going to find out about this," I said. "You know I'm going to tell them what I suspect. And with the glove and this break-in and the keys, they're going to have a lot of questions for you. For both of you."

"Oh my God!" Charles said.

"Shut up, Charles." Enid didn't take her eyes off me for even one second. "You don't have to tell them anything," she said. "Yes, I knew about that woman. And, yes, I was there that morning. But I didn't kill him. I swear it, Charles. He was alive when I left him." Her eyes shifted back to me. "We can make it worth your while to keep your mouth shut."

"No," I said.

"I know about you," Enid said. "I know your background. We can get you a new job—a better job. We can help you get qualified to practice law here."

I stared at her. Did she really think she could bribe me to cover up a murder?

"Enid, we should go," Charles said. "We should—"

I edged toward the kitchen table to get my purse and my phone.

"Stop her, Charles," Enid cried.

When Charles didn't make a move, Enid grabbed my arm. I tried to break free of her, but she shoved me backward. She was stronger than she looked. I tripped over a chair, crashed into a wall and crumpled to the floor. Something cracked under me. My ankle.

"Enid, please," Charles said. His face was white and he was sweating.

Enid's eyes went to the MedicAlert bracelet on my wrist. She glanced at the inhaler on my kitchen counter.

"She's allergic to artificial scents," she said mostly to herself. She turned toward me. "It must be a pretty bad allergy if you need that bracelet and an inhaler. I hear people can die from those allergy attacks." She reached for her purse and pulled out a small spray vial.

"What are you doing?" Charles asked.

"She can make things look bad for us, Charles. If she tells the police that I was at the house—"

"That you were *both* at the house," I said. My eyes were fixed on the spray vial. What was she going to do?

"If she tells them about the keys," Enid continued, "that little tramp might get away with it. You don't want that to happen, do you? You don't want us to get arrested, do you?"

"For what?" Charles said. "You said you didn't do anything. *I* didn't do anything."

"Look around you, Charles," Enid said.

"I wasn't at the house. I didn't do anything."

"Yes, you did," I said. "You broke in here and attacked me. You're helping her. Even if you didn't kill your father, the police will charge you will being an accessory after the fact—and that's in addition to charges of break-and-enter, assault, forcible confinement and—" I looked at the perfume vial in Enid's hand and the desperate look on her face. "And attempted murder, if not murder," I added.

Enid came toward me. I tried to get up, but pain shot up through my leg. My ankle was broken. I was sure of it.

"Things are bad enough for you two, Charles," I said. "I know Enid wasn't alone in the house. I know a man was there. I smelled cologne. I had a reaction to it."

"I wasn't there," Charles wailed.

"It was the old man," Enid said. "That's what you smelled."

"No, it wasn't," I told her. "I checked. Mr. Camden let me back into the house. I smelled all the cologne Mr. Withers had. There was no match. Mr. Camden knows what I suspect. I told him."

Enid hand's sagged a little. For the first time, she seemed unsure of herself.

"I went to a store. I found the cologne I smelled that morning," I said. "It's in that bag." I nodded to the counter. "I called Detective Bodie. I left him a message. I asked him to come by and get it. I told him what I suspected. If anything happens to me, he'll come after you."

Charles grabbed the department store bag and ripped it open. He pulled out the bottle of cologne and stared at it in astonishment. He held it up to Enid. Her face went pale.

"This is the same cologne that Andrew wears," Charles said. "What did you two do, Enid?"

Enid was staring at the small bottle too.

"No," she said weakly. "No."

Someone hammered on my door.

"Ms. Suarez?" called a familiar voice. "Ms. Suarez, it's Detective Bodie."

# CHAPTER TWELVE

"I'm here," I called to Bodie. "So are Enid and Charles Withers. They broke in and assaulted me." I looked at Charles. His face was chalky white. "If you don't let him in, he'll break the door down. Things will be even worse for you."

Charles walked slowly to the door and unlocked it. Bodie stood in the hall, his gun in his hand. Charles raised his hands instantly. Enid did the same. Bodie called for backup.

"Are you okay, Ms. Suarez?" Bodie asked.

"I think my ankle is broken."

Bodie called an ambulance. While we waited, I told him what had happened.

"There's been a terrible mistake," Charles said. "I can explain."

"You'll get your chance," Bodie said.

The other police and the ambulance arrived at almost the same time. The police took Charles and Enid into custody. The ambulance took me to the hospital.

* * *

It was late that night before I was ready to leave the hospital on crutches with my ankle in a cast. To my surprise, Bodie was waiting for me.

"Are you okay?"

"My ankle is broken. I'll be on crutches for six weeks." That meant I wouldn't be able to work. I didn't know how I was going to be able to pay my rent. "What happened to Charles and Enid? And Andrew?"

"They're all under arrest—Andrew for the murder of his father."

"What?" I couldn't believe my ears. "Andrew killed Charles? When did that happen?"

"Charles isn't the father," Bodie said. "He's the stepfather. Richard Withers is the father."

"*What?*"

"That was pretty much my reaction," Bodie said. "It seems Enid had an affair with Richard while Richard's wife was still alive. Enid got pregnant. The old man gave her an allowance, but he refused to divorce his wife. She got back at him by going after Charles—Richard's only other child—and marrying him instead. When Richard found out, he told her that if she said anything to anyone, he would cut Charles out of his will. Charles wouldn't inherit a dime. Neither would she or Andrew."

"That's pretty harsh," I said.

Bodie nodded. "Well, you *have* met the woman," he said.

I saw his point. Enid Withers was a difficult woman to like.

"According to Enid," he continued, "the old man took great delight in telling her that he was going to marry Maria. Enid was furious. She argued with him. But there was nothing she could do."

"Except kill him so that he wouldn't change his will after he got married," I said.

"He'd already changed it. But she didn't know that. She also didn't know that he'd included a provision for the baby. It must have been hard for her when she found out—especially after the way the old man treated her son."

"Did she confess?"

Bodie shook his head. "She says she didn't do it. She says he was alive when she left the house. Andrew is backing her up."

"And you believe him?"

"I do," Bodie said. "We finally found a couple of witnesses. Someone saw Enid arrive at the house just before eight in the morning. She parked right in the driveway. Someone else saw a car matching the description of Andrew's car pull up a few minutes later. He parked around the corner, as if he didn't want anyone seeing him. A man out walking his dog saw him enter through the side of the property. And as far as we've been able to tell, his car was still parked around the corner after Enid drove away. So it's possible that Andrew and Enid are telling the truth. It's possible Enid wasn't involved."

"Did Andrew say anything else?"

"He told us his side of the story. Did you know he was in love with Maria?"

"Yes."

Bodie frowned. "Exactly how much information did you withhold from the police, Ms. Suarez?" he asked.

"I just found out about Andrew this morning, from Maria. I was going to tell you."

He looked far from convinced.

"Andrew says he went to the house to see Maria," he said. "He was obsessed with her. He says he loved her and that he wanted to beg her to give him another chance. Instead, he ended up talking to the old man, who told him that he was going to marry Maria. He says that's when he lost control of himself. He grabbed the first thing he laid hands on and smashed the old man over the head. He killed his own father and didn't even know it. Enid hid it from him—and from Charles."

"So Andrew confessed?" I asked.

Bodie nodded.

"Then Maria is free to go?" I asked.

"She'll be released tomorrow." He glanced at his watch. "Better make that this morning. Can I give you a lift home, Ms. Suarez?"

He not only drove me home, but he also helped me up to my apartment.

I slept for a couple of hours before being woken by my phone. It was Maria.

"I'm free!" she crowed. "That detective, he said it's because of you."

"I think he had a lot to do with it too, Maria."

"I am going tomorrow to see Mr. Richard's lawyer," she said. "He says there are many details to take care of. Will you come with me, Connie? I want to understand everything he says."

I told her I would be happy to go with her.

"And, Connie, I talked to Mr. Camden about you. I told him I want to help you become a lawyer here in this country. He says he can tell us what to do. I will help you, Connie. I can do that now."

"What will I tell Mike?" I asked with a laugh.

"You tell him what I told him. You tell him, 'Mike, I quit.'"

I had to admit, it sounded like a great idea. I could hardly wait.

**NORAH McCLINTOCK**'s fascinating mysteries are hard to put down. She is a five-time winner of the Crime Writers of Canada's Arthur Ellis Award for Best Juvenile Crime Novel. Norah grew up in Montreal, Quebec, and now lives with her family in Toronto, Ontario. Visit www.web.net/~nmbooks for more information.